MONTE'S MISFITS: TOILET PAPER AND TRETCHERY

SUSAN CADY ALLRED PEGGY CADY KENDALL
C.G. CADY NAEGLE

For our families who have stuck by us through hours of writing well into the night, listening to our stories, and allowing us to go on multiple weekend trips disguised as "writing retreats"—opportunities to strengthen our relationships with one another and our memories of our parents. We are truly blessed.

Other Monte's Misfits Books

Monte's Misfits: The Magically Messy Mayhem of Growing Up With Ten Kids

Monte's Misfits—Ten Kids No Kidding!

Monte's Misfits: Creative Parenting

Monte's Misfits: Ho Ho Holy Christmas Chaos!

Contents

Introduction

For as long as I can remember, the first thing out of anyone's mouth after they found out I had nine siblings was, "Are you Catholic?"

"No."

"Are you Mormon?"

"Actually, yes."

But that's not why our parents had so many of us. Our father was an only child for the first ten years of his life to a mother who resented him, and our mother had only one brother. Dad was often left alone and felt unwanted. Mom, being an Army brat who travelled from city to city throughout her childhood, often felt alone.

When he and Mom got married, Dad was adamant that she would stay home with the kids so the children were never alone. He promised to do whatever it took to make sure it could be that way. And he did.

We never, in all the years they were married, doubted how much our father loved our mother. Or us.

As a result of the parenting plan, our parents often had to resort to creative ways to make ends meet, and responsibilities of childrearing and cleaning were spread out amongst everyone, depending on their ages. But they made it work, we always felt loved, and we never went without.

Toilet Paper and Treachery offers a series of stories about one of our favorite family past times from three different perspectives, often weaving memories of the same incident between the stories but through different eyes.

We hope you enjoy reading these stories as much as we had fun writing them.

Sincerely,

The Crazy Cady Sisters,
Chris, Peggy, Susan, and Cathy

P.S. If you want to purchase more of our stories, you can find them at: amzn.to/2yPrP5V

ONE

The Dogs Are Barking Tonight

WRITTEN BY PEGGY

Lynnwood, Washington
Summer, 1983

His feet crashed like thunderbolts as he ran down the stairs two-at-a-time. Where was he headed? Towards me. I was in his room. It's ok, I was supposed to be there. I was working for him, shredding newspaper as thin as I could. Then again, he was working for me, so I guess we were working together.

"I got it!" Chuck said with a huge grin, eyes dancing with mischief. "They aren't going to know what hit them! I'd like to see them top this one." Chuck was tall with dark, curly hair he controlled by keeping it cut short. He tended to have a serious face, was quiet, and mostly enjoyed doing things with, of all people, his sisters. And this weekend he was all mine!

What did he get? Twenty-four rolls of toilet paper. Why was I shredding newspaper? Woo Hoo! We were going TPing tonight!! This was no ordinary TP project. We were on a mission. My best friend, Jenny, was spending the night. Her boyfriend, Max, was spending the night at Jake's house.

Jake was a great guy. He laughed easily, was fun to be with, and liked a challenge. This weekend we were the challenge. Jake had heard about one of our TPing escapades and said he didn't think we'd be able to TP his house without being caught. "Excu-u-use me?" I said with one eyebrow raised. "What is so special about your house?"

"Oh nothing. Except if I know you're coming, I'll be up looking to catch you."

Being fifteen and 'all that,' both Jenny and I responded, "I don't think so! You could have all your friends spending the night and we could probably hit you undetected."

Game on.

A sinister grin spread across my face as I mentally shook myself and refocused on my task: shredding newspaper by hand. The steady, monotonous sound of "Shwip. Shwip. Shwip," floated out the bedroom door and into the family room. Continuous, never ending, annoying, "Shwip. Shwip. Shwip."

Jenny made paper punch holes. How do you do that? Exactly as you would expect; by taking a hole puncher and punching holes in paper and extricating the holes from the compartment beneath. It was a monotonous job, but we were on a mission and that mission included shredding as much newspaper and making as many hole punches as we could in sixty minutes.

That was all the time we got before we had to move to the next task. We had a schedule and we had an agenda. We knew exactly what we were doing and the precise time allotted to each segment of our onslaught in order to travel, traumatize, and retreat. Shred newspaper, punch holes, string toilet paper, fork the grass, soap the car windows, and if we had time, eat a package of Oreos and leave the empty container on the steps before retreating into the darkness undetected. Cruel you say? Yes. We gave cruel a new meaning.

The pitter-patter of tiny feet ebbed and the whining of tired babies quieted. Excitement hung in the air. Soon I heard the quiet drone of news and knew that the younger ones followed tradition and fell asleep watching TV. This was confirmed with one quick peek beyond the door frame. Small bodies in varying levels of dress lay sprawled across the couch and floor with eyes closed, trying to mimic the sound of Mom coming through the heat vents.

Wow! Could she snore! Put her and Dad together and it's a wonder the roof was still on the house.

Heavy footsteps came down the stairs. Dad was coming to check in before going to bed.

Jenny froze, her eyes widening slightly. "Oh crap! Your dad is coming. What's he going to do?"

I snorted. "Nothing. He loves this stuff. As long as he

knows where we are going and what we are doing, he'll be fine." That was one of the cool things about Dad. During the summer, as long as we got our chores done, followed the most important rules, and were ready on time for church Sunday morning, we had the freedom to do mostly what we wanted.

"OK," Jenny said hesitantly as she put her head down and started furiously punching holes to avoid eye contact with Dad as his huge frame filled the doorway.

"What are you trouble makers up to?" he asked with mock seriousness.

"Shredding newspaper," I said nonchalantly.

"I can see that," he grumped. "And why might you be shredding newspaper at...11:45 at night?"

"Well," I slowly started and then dove into my explanation. "Max is spending the night at Jake's house tonight and Jake said that there's no way that we could TP his house without them knowing about it and we couldn't let that challenge go unanswered, so not only are we going to TP his house, we are going to fork it, soap the cars, and spread newspaper and hole punches all over the grass. It will be the best hit EVER! And Chuck said he would drive."

"Hmm," Dad said after a brief moment. He looked at Jenny who was furiously trying to be invisible and asked, "Do your folks know about this?"

She stopped what she was doing and put on a confident smile, "Well, they know that I'm spending the night here and I'm pretty sure I mentioned something about going TPing, so I'm sure they're fine with it."

Dad "Hrmphed," and gave us, and our stuff, one last look before saying, "Alright. Don't do anything stupid."

"OK," I said and went back to work.

Jenny looked at me, then at the empty doorway, and back to me and said in amazement, "Is that all?"

I shrugged. "Yep. He thinks all this is funny...until the Robinson's get TPd, then he gets grumpy. Something about it not being their fault they live next to a house full of rowdy teenagers."

1:00 a.m. arrived, and all the goods were loaded into the back of our circa 1972 station wagon. Its wood-grained side panels were not pretty to look at, but the Blue Bomber had helped us safely execute many an exciting adventure.

Tonight would be no exception. Well, except the muffler was blown on it...again. That's ok, though. We just upped our game of stealth and parked two blocks away, around the corner, facing down hill to facilitate our fast escape. We didn't think twice about hauling garbage bags full of our spoils towards our target. And so it began.

The lights were off throughout the entire house, but we knew the boys were in the t.v. room which faced the driveway. This called for covert operations. Good thing we were dressed all in black. I even had a black cap on with my blonde hair tucked inside. After all, this was serious stuff!

We started with the toilet paper around the bushes surrounding the front of the house. Next we threw the rolls up into the trees and watched them fall to the ground with quiet, "thump"s as they formed white waterfalls flowing from the trees.

This left the most visual impact the fastest. Next came the hole punches. These would leave the greatest impression for the longest period of time. We threw them on the lawn like we were feeding chickens in a barnyard, all the while keeping our eyes on the windows as we looked for moving curtains. Next it was the newspaper. That was when it happened.

"CAR!" Chuck hissed as loudly as he could.

That was our signal to hide because a car was coming. We all dove behind the side of the house as a car pulled onto the street and slowed as it passed the house. Who wouldn't slow seeing all that white billowing from the trees, bushes, and lawn. Especially if that car was a police car. And it was.

The car creeped down the street and stopped in front of Jake's house. One of the officers got out with his flashlight and shone it around the front yard. In the silence of the night we could hear the conversation between the two of them. "Oh man! You gotta check this out!"

"Whoa!" said the second officer. "This place got nailed! I wonder how long it took?"

"I dunno," said the first officer, "but with all that paper, I'm betting they are long gone."

They admired the yard for a few more minutes before getting back into their vehicle and slowly driving off.

We looked at each other and slowly let out a collective sigh of relief. Now what? Do we keep going or is there a chance that they might come back? After a brief exchange, we decided if they were going to come back, it wouldn't be right away and we needed to kick it into turbo speed so our efforts wouldn't be wasted. WE HAD TO COMPLETE THE CHALLENGE!

Very quickly we spread the newspaper, stabbed the forks through the newspaper into the grass, soaped down the windows of the cars, and instead of leaving a package of empty Oreos on the porch, opened them and adhered them to the soapy windows.

as we were applying the final cookies, Jenny hissed, "CAR!" and we all ran to the side of the house and peeked around the corner. Our secret admirers had returned, only this time they brought friends.

Two police cars stopped in front of the house and one officer got out of each car. "See!" the one officer said to the other, laughter filling his voice. "I've never seen a TP job like this. It's like a blizzard hit."

The second officer turned his head to look at the first one, obviously not amused. "Someone's not going to be happy in the morning. Let's spread out and take a look."

The three of us looked at each other and silently mouthed, "OH CRAP!" at the same time.

I pointed to the back yard.

We crawled on our hands and knees and found some bushes close to the house. We sat between them with our backs to the wall and waited.

As the minutes ticked by I started thinking of all the things that would happen if we got caught. I thought of everything from being grounded for the rest of my life to getting kicked out of Driver's Ed and never being given a license. I leaned forward and put my head in my arms on the dirt and tried to melt into the ground. Everything got really quiet and the next thing I knew, I was waking up to a dog's wet snout sniffing my face and a bright light in my eyes.

"What are you kids doing back here?" a gruff, male voice asked.

"Umm. TPing my boyfriend and his friend's house," Jenny timidly replied.

"Do they know that you are out here?" the voice asked.

"Well they should since they dared us to do it," Jenny said.

"Hmm," he said. "There have been a series of break ins in the neighborhood, so we had to wake up his parents. They are in the front so let's find out if they want to press charges. Let's go."

He escorted us to the front of the house where a visibly

perturbed Mr. and Mrs. Eliott stood in the front yard in their pajamas.

Max and Jake, on the other hand, were in total awe at the deluge of white that filled the yard. "Wow!" Max said as we came around the corner. "We fell asleep waiting for you to come. This is amazing!"

"I hope you boys feel the same way as you spend the morning cleaning it up," said Mr. Eliott.

"I can come help in the morning since I helped to make the mess," Jenny said cheerfully.

"I think you've done enough," replied Mr. Eliott.

"OK. Well, since I won't be here tomorrow, can I sign your bathroom wall right now?"

Seriously? Now was not the time to carry on the tradition of signing their bathroom wall the first time you came to visit.

All eyes turned to Jenny as she sheepishly shrugged her shoulders, "I have a feeling it will be a long time before I get to come over again, and I wanted to sign your wall before it is all filled up."

Mrs. Eliott moaned as she took Jenny inside to leave her signature for the world to see.

After we pulled into the carport of our house and tried to avoid the squeaky stairs of the porch, I quietly made my way to Dad and Mom's bedroom to let them know we were home.

I poked my head into their room and was greeted by Dad's sleepy voice saying, "So they didn't lock you up, huh?"

I froze for a second and innocently said, "What do you mean?"

Without bothering to move he said, "We got a call from the police a couple of hours ago asking if I knew where our car was."

"Uhuh," I slowly answered.

"I told them 'Yes, my kids have it out TPing,' and asked if there was a problem." Right about then I stopped breathing, but Dad just kept on going.

"The officer said there wasn't a problem except the car was found illegally parked a couple of blocks away from a neighborhood that had had a series of break ins. He mentioned something about a K-9 unit scouring the area so I told them to call me if you needed picked up at the station." He yawned a huge yawn and continued, "You are home, so I assume they didn't lock you up."

After a brief pause and a prayer of thanks thrown in the direction of heaven I replied, "Thanks Dad. Glad you didn't lose any sleep over it."

"Nope," he said. "I told you not to do anything stupid so I assumed you wouldn't. Let's talk about it in the morning. G'night."

TWO

What Goes Up, Must Come Down

WRITTEN BY CATHY

Lynnwood, Washington
1987

"It's time to get up! It's time to get up! It's time to get up in the morning!"

I groaned angrily and pulled my pink striped blanket tight over my head, wrapping the rest of it around me in an attempt to block out Dad's bright tenor.

He was at the top of the stairs. His singing floated to the bottom, then attacked the inhabitants of the two large bedrooms at the base.

I squeezed my eyelids shut, blatantly ignoring my inevitable rise from bed.

The heat of my breath in the confined space became unbearable. I burrowed my finger into the blankets at my face, trying to create a path for fresh air without making any movement that might betray my state of consciousness. The worming worked, and I sucked in a mouthful of cool air before the tunnel collapsed.

My six years of life flashed before me while I slowly suffocated.

Creaking stairs interrupted the fantasies of my imminent death as Dad's 6'2" frame lumbered down them.

I quickly weighed my options. I could either sit here in musty misery dreaming against all hope and known history Dad would change his mind and let us continue sleeping. Or I could get up and face Saturday morning chores head-on, and hope my obedience would be looked at favorably.

Even at my young age, I understood the cruel mistress of reality. Each step Dad descended increased the displeasure he felt toward having to follow up on his good morning "Reveille" song.

Moisture accumulated on my upper lip. Bursting out of my cocoon with a dramatic gasp of air, I hit the ground running, hoping to reach Dad before he got more than halfway down the stairs.

I was successful, and I darted past him, pausing only to give him an ingratiating hug around the waist. No time for more, though. That squeeze made either my tummy or his grumble, and I realized I was famished!

Dad rumbled downstairs waking the other siblings, eliciting a murmur of voices, especially the teenager ones.

I tried to decipher their conversation with one ear as I crawled on top of the counter to get a cereal bowl.

Dad's voice wasn't particularly angry - I must have assuaged him with my obedience - but I did sense a sort of admonition to it. The olders (Patty, Susan, Matt, and Peggy), protested, but I couldn't hear what through the rattle of my Tasty-O's being poured into the warped plastic bowl. I scooped two heaping spoonfuls of sugar onto the bland generic oat cereal then covered it with milk.

The sound doesn't muffle Dad's, "Well check it out for yourself!" and the pounding of feet running up the stairs.

I anticipated the herd of olders to ascend at any moment into the kitchen. Picking up the pace, I shoveled the cereal into my mouth and tryed to figure out if I could inhale it quickly enough to get a second bowl before the food was gone.

But they stopped at the landing of our split-level home and pulled the front door open. The olders crowded onto the porch landing just outside.

The silence roared in my ears, and I raised slightly off my seat to investigate the view through the picture window on the front of the house. My spoon stopped midway to my mouth, little bits of cereal dribbling out of it.

What I saw outside caused me to do the unthinkable: I left the kitchen table where my yummy, edible food sat, and dashed to the window.

Our yard, with trees and cars and porches and toys,

appeared the same as always: a little tattered, well played in, but in its natural state.

The neighbor's yard, though, was covered in strips of long white toilet paper. It was wrapped around trunks, tossed over their large trees, enveloped outdoor lamps, and suffocated rose bushes. The morning dew caused it to cling to everything it touched, promising disintegration if a removal attempt were initiated. Stray strands fluttered in the morning air. The TP job was almost beautiful, if it wasn't so ugly.

Poor Mr. Robinson stood in the middle of the yard shaking his head and trying to clean up his once-pristine landscape.

The Robinsons were a nice retired couple living next door to a family with ten wild kids. His home was sandwiched between our family and the Collins, who had a daughter, Kimmie, that Susan, Patty, and Becca adored.

To this day, I'm not sure whose friend Kimmie really was. I think it was Susan, but Susan's entourage of little sisters was a package deal. In order to get to Kimmie's house, we scampered down the hill of our driveway, dashed past the Robinson's yard, then trudged back up the hill to Kimmie's house.

No way were we allowed to cross the Robinson's yard to get to Kimmie's. Who cared if the prescribed way was three times longer. We were not allowed to get caught in the Robinson's yard, and that was that.

The sad part was, this wasn't the first time the poor, innocent Robinson had been TP-ed. Or the second. Or the last.

We lived in a suburb of Seattle filled with cookie-cutter homes. Unfortunately, the Robinson's and our house plans were identical, so it wasn't shocking the two houses were mistaken for each other in the pre-dawn darkness.

Dad's voice was low but firm as he nudged the kids down the stairs.

Their response was immediate and slightly harried. They dashed down the stairs and over the asphalt driveway, oblivious to the bits of rock digging into their bare feet.

As the spokesperson, Peggy humbly approached Mr. Robinson, whose face was still a mask of astonishment.

I couldn't hear what they discussed, but there was general arm waving, nodding, and unintelligible gesticulation.

After Peggy placed a reassuring hand on Mr. Robinson's arm, he shuffled back into his house, shaking his head and scratching his whiskers.

When his front door closed, Peggy's face hardened and she started directing. Susan got to work on the bushes and around the trees. Matt took the roses. Patty returned from our house dragging rakes and other long poles to each of her siblings.

This wasn't their first time at the rodeo, and in quick order the easily accessible toilet paper created a pile in the middle of the well-manicured yard.

The four of them gently maneuvered their respective poles attempting to evict the high-rise papers. The day hadn't burned off the morning dew, and each poke or nudge doubled the number and halved the size of the toilet paper.

Eventually they gave up, and Peggy promised Mr. Robinson they would return when the paper dried.

By the time the olders gathered the piles of toilet paper into their arms, Becca began stirring downstairs.

I catapulted off the couch and slopped my now-soggy food into my mouth, simultaneously reaching for the cereal box.

Becca groggily stumbled into the kitchen, her face creased with pillow marks. "Where is everyone?"

"They're outside cleaning up the Robinson's yard. They got TP-ed again."

She nodded vaguely, nonplussed, and proceeded to get to the business of filling her tummy.

~

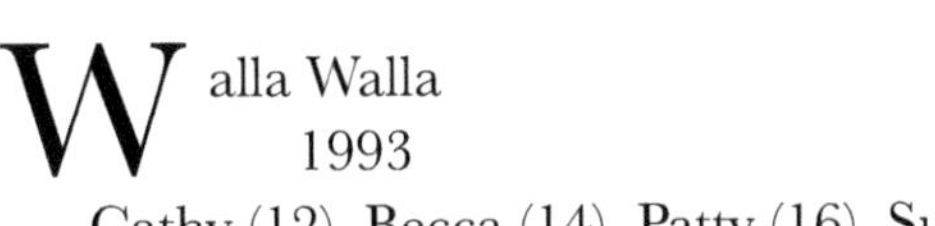

Walla Walla
1993
Cathy (12), Becca (14), Patty (16), Susan (18)

Years passed, and I was finally at the precipice of being able to go toilet papering with my sisters.

They'd snuck me out a time or two and I'd tossed a few misappropriated rolls myself. It was exciting. It was exhilarating. It took effort!

Who knew there was a certain skill to throwing a roll of toilet paper into a tree and not getting it stuck?

My first time out, I was allocated two rolls, and after two throws I was done for the night.

But this night, Mom and Dad would be gone overnight. This allowed for the deliciousness of staying up late, eating ice cream, and watching *Girls Just Want to Have Fun* or *The Princess Bride.*

Fast asleep on the couch, I was gently tugged into semi-consciousness by some unknown interruption.

With effort, I pulled my heavy eyes open.

Through the picture window at the front of the house, I saw Patty's friend, Cameron, crouching on the large, walk-out porch. His body pressed against the raised flower beds forming the wall separating the rock garden covered by the roof with the rhododendron bushes and lawn beyond.

My torpid mind registered curiosity, but my eyes wrestled control of themselves and dropped closed again.

I hadn't slept long when murmuring voices floated through the screen door into the house. I opened my eyes again and was stupefied that Cameron had changed into a police officer talking to Patty.

Having been awoken twice by Patty and/or her friends, I was disproportionately angry with the situation. I was also too punchy to do anything about it, so I just rolled over with an indignant a huff, and fell asleep with my nose against the back of the couch.

I woke up in the morning to the sound of our screen door slamming. The sun touched the horizon, flashing streaks of light into our hidden garden outside the dining room.

Susan, Patty, and Becca had just filed outside, Becca making sure to let the screen crash so I could wake up and participate in the dark side of toilet papering.

Now that I was a semi-active TP participant, regardless of how minor my part, I was obligated to help clean it up. They had already done the vast majority of the work last night.

Apparently Cameron and the police were not a dream.

As normal for the youngest, I missed all the excitement!

My task was to climb high into the pine trees. This way I could extract any stragglers that might hint to the parents any mischief may have occurred while they were away.

Some of the trees were unclimbable, but there was one tree I could get to. It was on the corner of our lot, one side facing a main thoroughfare, 2nd Avenue, and the other side on Stone Street.

I wrestled my way up the branches, my legs etched white with scrapes and my hands sticky with sap.

Becca handed me a broom handle, and I clumsily held it three fingers of my right hand.

As I climbed, I gripped the branches with the thumb and pointer finger, trying to keep the excessive sap from getting on the broom handle.

I stopped about fifteen feet up. Wrapping my left arm around the trunk, I gripped the handle in my right arm.

I looked up and down 2nd Avenue hoping for a break in the traffic, keenly aware of how humiliating it was to be fifteen feet up a tree flailing a broomstick at toilet paper lodged within said tree.

Who does this? Why, the Cady's of course.

Traffic was scarce, but about two blocks down I saw a pair of pedestrians walking up the sidewalk toward us. That was motivation enough for me. I didn't care how much I was flailing, I was getting that cursed toilet paper down!

And flail I did.

"Slow down, Cathy! You're ripping it!"

The dew had settled, and the toilet paper was doing the thing that set it apart from all other papers: disintegrating.

My eyes flickered to the pair coming our way, appalled at the clip they were going. One of them was a young child. Shouldn't the mother compensate for his short legs?

In spite of my frustration and embarrassment, thoughts of Mom and Dad seeing any evidence in the trees slowed me, and I extracted the first layer of toilet paper. I moved up two branches and began work on next layer when I heard a young voice below me.

"What's she doing, Mommy?"

"She's cleaning up the toilet paper."

Now they decide to slow down?

"But how did it get up there?"

"Um... well... her friends put it up there."

"Her friends?" The dismay in the little boy's voice was real. "Why would friends do that? That doesn't seem very nice."

They meandered out of my hearing range, so I couldn't hear the mother's explanation. That didn't stop me from thinking about it, though. Why would friends do this?

I thought of my sisters' group of friends, and couldn't suppress my smile at the fun they had pranking each other.

And I couldn't wait until I was old enough to do this to my own friends.

THREE

Toilet Paper and Treachery

WRITTEN BY SUSAN

Lynnwood, Washington
1989

My childhood never included cell phones, video chat, Netflix, or the Internet. None of that showed up until after I was married. My childhood consisted of (gasp!) entertaining myself.

One such activity I remember a lot of was toilet papering (or TPing). For those who don't know what TPing is, you buy several dozen rolls of toilet paper, go to a person's house in the middle of the night, and throw the rolls into their trees, over their house, their cars, or any animals dumb enough to sit still and take the abuse. If done right, the victim's home may look like a blizzard hit in the middle of August.

Provided you aren't cruel enough to TP a person's home in the middle of a rainstorm, when there's snow already on the ground, or during a windstorm, TPing is relatively innocuous. Annoying as all-get-out for the person who has to clean it up, but still harmless.

Being the seventh child, I spent a lot of time waking up to our house (or our neighbor's house, if the perpetrators had the wrong address – which happened often) being TPed.

Those were the mornings Dad stormed into our rooms singing Reveille at the top of his lungs. He stomped around and gave us five minutes to get our butts out of bed and onto the front lawn to clean up the mess.

I heard stories from the older kids about past toilet papering escapades, and who they were planning to get next.

I spent years asking to tag along, but the family rule required a child to be at least twelve-years-old to TP.

After several agonizing years of waiting, I finally came of age. However, this also occurred after a certain incident involving K-9 units, the police, and my parents being called in the middle of the night.

I didn't have the opportunity to do anyone's house until just before we moved from our home in Lynnwood, Washington.

As soon as Mom and Dad told us we'd be moving, I started saving money. I had a few friends I'd grown up with, and I wanted to to leave an impression when I left. By golly, this was going to be the *best* TP job of all time!

It would be epic.

I don't know who I got to drive us. I was only fourteen, after all. Bless them for doing it. I was a girl on a mission, and I wasn't going to stop with one house.

The first house on my list? Mark.

We grew up together. Some of my earliest memories were playing in his basement while my older siblings hung out upstairs.

He was pretty cool, but a bit annoying. From an adult perspective, I think he probably wanted attention. As a kid, I just wanted to tackle and beat on him. Which I did. More often than I care to admit.

Aside from my best friend, Kimmie, Mark was the friend I would miss the most. That meant I'd pound his house the hardest. That's how we Cadys show our love, right?

I spent the next month doing chores, babysitting, saving money, fishing through couch cushions, checking pockets in the laundry, and begging my mother for extra coins so I could buy toilet paper. I shopped the newspaper ads, looking for the best deals. I wanted the biggest bang for my buck.

When it came time to do our magic, there were five of us. Somehow, Becca convinced Mom she was old enough to come along. She was only ten. Ugh. The younger kids get away with everything!

Kimmie came with us, saving herself from being a TP victim.

No one ever accused Kimmie of being stupid.

We drove over to Mark's house and parked at the end of the cul-de-sac.

Darkness filled the landscape aside from a streetlight creating a bright beam on the road that gradually faded to darkness the further you got from the center. A single bulb illuminated Mark's front porch, but all the windows were dark.

A dog barked, alerting the world of our presence.

We waited, hidden in the shadows, clothed entirely in black.

No one came to investigate.

My mouth watered. Look at the size of the trees in Mark's yard! Oh yeah. They'd be fishing toilet paper out of their branches for weeks!

I stayed out front, while a couple people ran around back. We waited till rolls of toilet paper sailed over the apex of the house, long, white tails fluttering in the air like a kite's. The toilet paper rolled downward, off the roof into the yard.

Move! Move! Move!

Our TPing party bolted into action, throwing rolls over the house and waiting for someone to throw them back, each pass covering the roof a little bit more. Behind us, others attacked the trees. They'd chuck their rolls as high into the branches as possible, then watched them flutter to the ground, leaving a trail of white draped over the leaves.

Occasionally, I checked the windows to see if anyone was watching.

At one point, we scattered, thinking we'd been discovered. False alarm.

We continued for several minutes until our allotment of toilet paper—several dozen rolls—disappeared. Standing at the end of the street, we marveled at a job well done.

Mark's house, covered entirely in white, nearly glowed in the moonlight. We high-fived each other, and climbed into the car, ready to attack the next house.

Walla Walla, Washington
April 1993

After we moved to Walla Walla, Washington word quickly spread that the Cady girls were not to be messed with. Occasionally, a few poor, unsuspecting fools tested that theory.

One such night occurred during my senior year of high school. My parents were out of town, and some of our friends caught wind of their departure.

It was nearly midnight and I was in the living room. I'd just arrived home from an eight-hour shift at the local Dairy Queen, and was sitting at the dining room table, in my ice-cream splattered uniform, talking to Patty.

We caught movement through our giant picture window facing the front yard. A red-headed body ran crouched past our our window. Cameron.

Patty and I exchanged look, a smile spreading over our faces, then bolted into action. The hunt was on!

Patty tore through the living room and out the front door.

I ran out the back door, hoping to circle around and flank them.

In the distance, Patty bellowed something, and one of our guy friends squealed like a little girl.

Silhouettes of heads passed me on the other side of our giant hedges.

I turned, mid-stride to follow them then hurtled through an opening in the hedges, narrowly missing one of the bodies shrouded in darkness.

They scattered like cockroaches. I picked one, Chris, hoping since he was the smallest of the group, he would be easiest to catch.

Oh, how I was wrong.

Chris glanced over his shoulder. Seeing me in pursuit, he turned on the speed, veering into a neighbor's front yard, and running behind their house and into another backyard. And then another.

I followed, losing the sneaky little bugger several blocks down the street. I stalked through several other backyards, hoping they didn't have a dog. Or a gun. And were asleep.

Fear snaked up my spine and the little hairs on my neck stood on end. After moving to the safety of the street, I stopping to listen. I glanced at the semi-familiar homes with well manicured lawns, trimmed bushes, and decorative fences. I was probably half a mile from home.

In the distance, Patty yelled. I bolted toward her, hoping to provide reinforcements. Not like she needed any. That girl was a tank. She could snap me like a twig.

Despite my being two years older than her--and a colonel in JROTC--Patty was two inches taller and a good thirty pounds of muscle heavier than me.

Halfway to her, I darted behind a tree. A police car passed at a crawl, as if looking for someone.

Images of my older sister, Peggy, being caught by a K-9 unit while TPing flashed through my head. What do the police do if they call home and nobody answers? Mom and Dad were out of town. Would we spend the weekend in jail?

I stayed close to the shadows, slowly making my way back to the house, avoiding two more police cars.

A cold sweat formed on my brow and the *Mission Impossible* theme song ran through my brain in a continuous loop. I resisted the urge to hum it out loud.

When I got home, Patty and Becca were out front, cleaning up toilet paper, forks, and various other treacherous methods of mayhem.

"The police were here," Patty said matter-of-factly over her shoulder, stuffing a giant pile of toilet paper into a black plastic leaf bag. "Someone from the neighborhood called about a noise complaint and people running in the streets. They went looking for you."

I grinned. "Yeah, I saw 'em. They didn't catch me though."

"Good. 'Cuz they weren't happy."

I spent the next hour helping my sisters pick up the mess the boys left behind. Hopefully Mom and Dad wouldn't notice we'd been Tied.

The three of us stood shoulder-to-shoulder in our front yard, our heads tilted toward the sky. White streams fluttered in the wind at the highest point of the tree.

Becca sighed. "Well, I guess we'll have to wait for the rain to disintegrate it."

"Those guys have quite the arm to get it that high," I marveled.

Patty frowned. "Dad won't be happy."

I shook my head. "Not much we can do about it though."

We trudged back into the house, leaving the stuffed garbage bags by the front door. We would put it by the trash can in the morning.

Even if we'd managed to get the toilet paper out of the tree, it wouldn't have mattered. We had wheat stalks growing in our grass and out of the hedges for years afterward, thanks to the boys and their little prank.

Little did they know, every time the stalks appeared, it reminded us it was time for more payback.

Never mess with the Cady sisters. We don't forget.

FOUR

Full Circle: Thing With a Husband

WRITTEN BY CATHY

Olympia, Washington
Summer 2017

Three of the four "Crazy Cady Sisters" are sitting at Chris's house working on our Monte's Misfits series.

Sitting around the cluttered wooden table, it feels like growing up. It has been a weekend of regimented work mingled with laughter and, let's not lie, food.

We talk about including a "full circle" story at the end, talking about how our childhood experiences impacted us as adults and as parents.

Ultimately, the full-circle stories are cut, but this one remains. Well, because it's one of our favorites.

We come to the chapter about TPing and are stumped as to who should write the full-circle.

My TPing days ended in college, and none of my kids are old enough to independently TP.

While the older sisters' kids have done TPing of their own, there isn't anything that stands out as memorable or funny.

I put on my big girl panties and decide to take one for the team. "Well, that means I get to make some toilet papering memories with my kids!"

With a twinkle in my eye, I immediately text my husband, Scott.

"We pitch the book to an agent in five weeks, and this is one of the chapters we're committing to having ready," Susan reminds me. "That means you've got to do the TPing, have it written, edited, and ready to go in that time."

My smile is mischievous, and the wheels are already turning. "I got this."

Once the girl's writing weekend is done, though, I am quickly wrapped up in the entrails of daily life, including hosting two exchange students for a month, one from

Japan and one from Korea. Five weeks seems like a long time, but I've barely blinked, and nearly two weeks pass. It is Wednesday night, and we are dropping the exchange students off at the airport in the morning.

I come home that evening from running my cub scouts meeting, I remind Scott of the need to go TPing.

"Okay. Let's get the Burbidges," he says.

"Right now? It's nearly 10 p.m. on a Wednesday night. I have to work in the morning, the kids need to finish packing, and do we have enough toilet paper in the house?" I say.

My husband shrugs. "Let's just get it out of the way."

Let's just get it out of the way?? Clearly my husband and I have somewhat different opinions about toilet papering.

We tell the kids what our final activity with the exchange students is and instruct them to hop in the minivan.

"Isn't this illegal, Dad?" ten-year old Tony pipes up immediately.

"If you are ethically opposed to it, you can stay behind. That's fine," Scot says.

Tony is the first one in the minivan. That's my boy.

After everyone else piles into the car, we head to the nearest grocery store. While I gas up, Scott buys the toilet paper.

Much to my chagrin, he exits with a twelve-roll pack of cheap toilet paper. The cheap wasn't the problem. I support cheap. There are only twelve rolls. That was the problem.

"That's two rolls of toilet paper per person," he explains. "That's plenty."

Clearly my husband and I have different opinions about toilet papering.

I roll my eyes and remind myself that I am grateful he's even coming. I steer the minivan toward our target, and Scott explains what's going on.

The exchange students are baffled. We're doing *what* with the toilet paper? And why? This is funny? Cole's and Bella's house? But they're our friends! Americans are crazy.

Once Scott explained the basics of draping our friend's yard in sheets of toilet paper, he lays out the rules: "We will NOT throw the toilet paper as high into the tree as we can… Tony." His pointed glare says it's actually for me. "We will NOT throw any rolls of toilet paper over the roof of the house… Tony." He continues to stare in my direction. "This is for fun. It should be easy for the Burbidges to get ALL the toilet paper picked up. They should be able to pick up faster than it took to be strewn about their yard… Tony."

I don't know who groaned more at this point, me or my ten-year-old.

Clearly my husband and I have very different opinions about toilet papering.

I park two blocks away from the Burbidges after only getting lost once. The Cady curse of getting lost in your own backyard is still strong in my adulthood.

Our horde of two adults, three teenagers and one tween walk down the dark road as nonchalantly as we can while brandishing a bright white roll of toilet paper glowing in each of our hands.

We're about halfway there when Scott hands me his rolls and motions for us to go on while he runs back to the minivan. He catches up with us holding a pair of tennis shoes and shorts. "They're Chad's (Tony's Burbidge counterpart). They've been in our car forever. I'll just leave them on their porch."

My harshly-whispered protestations are to no avail; he doesn't care if they know it's from us. He is sick of them sitting in our car.

Clearly my husband and I have radically different opinions about toilet papering.

When we arrive at the house, we hide behind the cars. The full-glass front door of their house shows nobody in the in-home beauty salon, but the entire rest of the house is lit up.

Surely the family is still awake. I tiptoe past the see-through door and peek my head into the front window. Through this window I see the living room, dining room, kitchen, and back door in the mud room. The ground floor is clear.

I give a thumbs up, and begin draping the front fence in sashes of soft white paper. I move to the bush in front of the window, covering it with even rows.

That is when the first car drives by.

The shouted whisper of, "Car!" is heard, and I hit the ground.

The exchange students look at me in bafflement, then at the other kids who had collapsed onto the dewy grass. They quickly follow suit.

Scott, on the other hand, continues wrapping his tree as the automobile rushes by.

Clearly my husband and I have extremely different opinions about toilet papering.

This happens a few more times, each car driving by more slowly than the one before. Finally, we are trapped in our hiding places for a few minutes while the Burbidge's neighbors arrive home and survey the damage with a chuckle.

This time Scott ends up hiding behind a bush. When

the neighbors retreat into their own home, he stretches and says it is time to go.

I wonder how much this decree coincides with the greater height I'm beginning to throw the rolls into the bushes.

"But we've still got four rolls left!" I protest. His response is a shrug and a gathering of the children.

Clearly my husband and I have horribly different opinions about toilet papering.

I stare at the full rolls of toilet paper in my hand, appeased by the fact that we will at least have four more rolls in the house.

As we're traipsing back to our vehicle, I notice Scott on the phone texting. Who in the world is he texting at this time of the night?

I sneak a peek over his shoulder and see his text just as it's being sent: "I left Chad's shoes and shorts on the porch."

He gets a good smack on the arm for that one. Returning stuff is one thing. Maybe they forgot who had possession of those. But to send a text? And at this time of the night? It's a dead giveaway.

"I wanted to make sure they weren't stolen from the porch."

C'mon, man! You're killing me.

No doubt about it, my husband and I have irreconcilable different opinions about toilet papering.

I go to bed that night satisfied I have fulfilled my duty to make TPing memories with my children. I thought the memory making was completed. Then I got home from work the next day and hear the rest of the story.

The story of Scott piling the kids into the car after I'd left for work so that they could help the Burbidges clean up the toilet paper from their yard.

Beyond a doubt, my husband and I have chasmic different opinions about toilet papering.

And it's probably good there's a little less crazy mixed into our family.

About Peggy Cady Kendall

CADY CHILD #4

Cady Kendall's love for writing sprouted when she was in elementary school and continued to grow through high school. This is when she took a creative writing class as an elective and learned to appreciate the power words had to invoke our five senses and heighten our emotions.

It wasn't until one of her sisters called with the idea to write "Monte's Misfits," that she began recording her childhood memories and giving them life through words. When she is not writing, Peggy is focused on her family, friends, gardening, and thinking of new projects to do around the house.

About Susan Cady Allred

CADY CHILD #7

Susan Cady Allred lives in Washington with her husband and two of her children. She prefers binge reading over binge-watching, enjoys the outdoors, and loves a good laugh. Some of Susan's fondest memories include reading till sunrise on school nights and scouring her family's hard-bound encyclopedia set for interesting facts. She writes mystery games at Whodunnitmysteries.com, has written four books about growing up in a family with ten kids, and writes stories about kids who face their demons head-on. To see more of what she writes, go to SusanCadyAllred.com.

facebook.com/susancadyallred
twitter.com/suzallredwriter
instagram.com/suzallredwriter
bookbub.com/profile/624255
goodreads.com/SusanCadyAllred

About C.G. Cady Naegle

CADY CHILD #10

Cathy (C.G. Cady Naegle) was born and raised in Washington State and she has also lived in Oregon and Alaska, so she considers herself a Pacific Northwest girl through and through.

She and her husband are the parents of three children, and her family has to compete for her attention far too much with her beagles, Roscoe and Mable. The story of when her four-year-old discovered that his mama loved him more than Roscoe will likely be in an upcoming book as an exemplification of what a fantastic mother she is.

In Cathy's real life (because writing these books has been a dream!) she works in Human Resources as a policy writer. That is much less exciting than sharing the exploits of her childhood.

She is also Head Mystery Game Writer at WhodunnitMysteries.com under the Pen Name Damien Lynch (because who's going to buy a mystery by a girl named Cathy?)

We Miss You Already!

Thank you for stopping by and spending some time with us!

We would LOVE to see you again. Please join us on social media so we can connect further.

Newsletter: bit.ly/2K5zMKY

Website: MontesMisfits.com

Facebook: Facbook.com/Montesmisfits/

Twitter: Twitter.com/montesmisfits

Instagram: instagram.com/montesmisfits

www.ingramcontent.com/pod-product-compliance
Ingram Content Group UK Ltd.
Pitfield, Milton Keynes, MK11 3LW, UK
UKHW022009190726
13853UKWH00004B/1837

9 798754 332782